Frustrated by a day full of teachers and classmates mispronouncing
her beautiful name, a little girl tells her mother she never wants
to go back to school. In response, the girl's mother teaches her
about the musicality of African, Asian, Black-American, Latinx, and
Middle Eastern names on their lyrical walk home through the city.
Empowered by this newfound understanding, the young girl is ready
to return the next day to share her knowledge with her class. *Your
Name is a Song* is a celebration that reminds us of the beauty, history,
and magic behind names.

This book came to you from
FIRST BOOK—
a nonprofit that provides
books & resources to scho
& community programs.
Discover more great titles
FirstBookMarketplace.or

SO-DZM-170

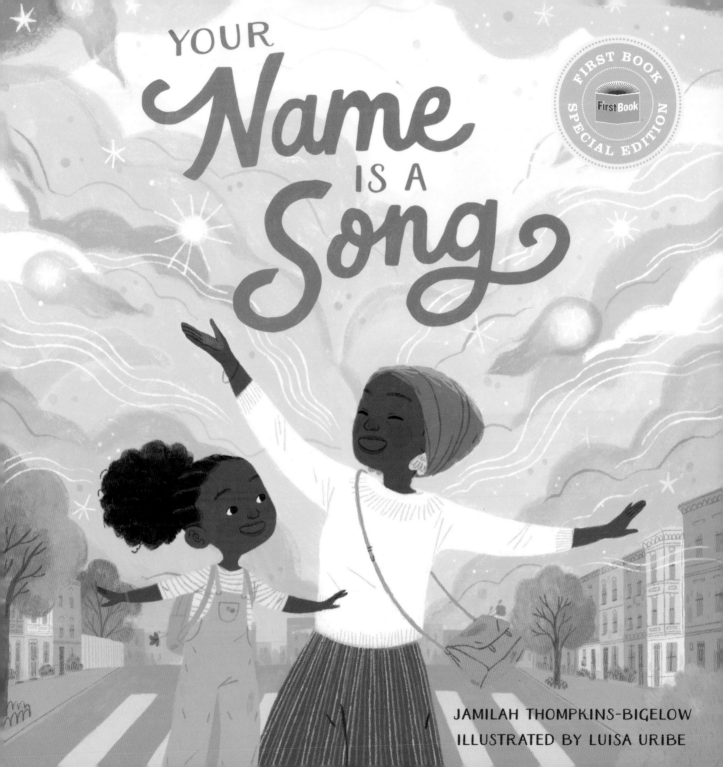

YOUR
Name
IS A
Song

JAMILAH THOMPKINS-BIGELOW
ILLUSTRATED BY LUISA URIBE

Stories for All

SPECIAL EDITION

brought to you by

To the griots of the past, present, and future.
Keep singing the important songs. — J.T-B.

For my mom. — L.U.

Library of Congress Control Number: 2019947277
ISBN 9781943147724

Text copyright © 2020 by Jamilah Thompkins-Bigelow
Illustrations by Luisa Uribe

Published by The Innovation Press
1001 4th Avenue, Suite 3200, Seattle, WA 98154
www.theinnovationpress.com

Printed and bound by Worzalla
Production date February 2020

Cover lettering by Nicole LaRue
Cover art by Luisa Uribe
Book layout by Tim Martyn

YOUR
Name
IS A
Song

JAMILAH THOMPKINS-BIGELOW ✦ ILLUSTRATED BY LUISA URIBE

"I'm not coming back ever again!" The girl stomped.

"Please don't stomp unless we're stepping in a drill team,"
Momma said. "Was your first day of school so bad?"
The girl looked down. "No one could say my name."

"No one? Not even your teacher?" Momma asked.

"She tried. It got stuck in her mouth."

A street musician swayed and played.

Momma closed her eyes until she swayed too.

"Tell your teacher that your name is a song."

The girl wrinkled her brows. "I can't say that! Names aren't songs!"

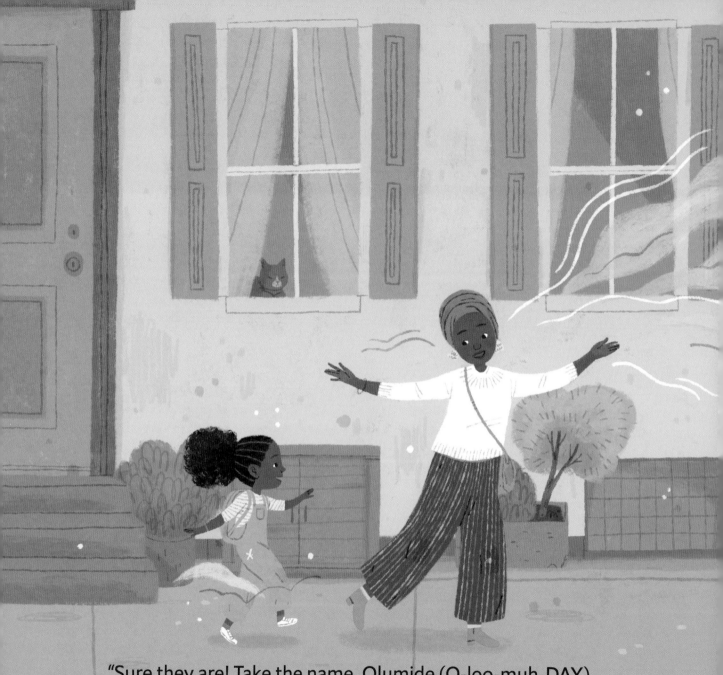

"Sure they are! Take the name, Olumide (O-loo-muh-DAY). Olumide is a melody, girl! And so is Kotone (KOH-tow-neh)."

The girl whispered names. *TAP-ta-TAP* went her feet. "Mamadou (MAW-muh-DOO) is a beat! Thandolwethu (TAHN-dol-WEH-tooh) stretches out like a love song!"

"Yes, girl! Names are songs. Sing your name.

Your teacher will learn to sing it too."

The girl did a jig as they walked on.

But then, her feet slowed.

"Ummi (OOM-mee)," she called to her momma. "During snack, some girls pretended to choke on my name."

At the red light, a car boomed hip-hop beside them. The bass pounded from their heads to their toes—even in their chests. *Pat! Pat! Pat!* Momma patted her chest. "Tell those girls some names must be said from here, not the throat."

"Names come from your heart?" the girl asked.

"Say the name Ha (HA) from there. You got to go deeper to say Ahlam (AH-Hlam)."

As they crossed, the girl touched her chest.

"Juana (HWAH-nah) is here. Ngozi (INN-GO-zee) goes deeper—
it pokes me in the stomach!"

"Yes, girl! From your heart, say your name. Those girls will learn
to use their hearts too."

The girl bopped to the beat as they walked on. "In art, one boy's eyes got all wide when I said my name! Is my name scary?"

Wires sparked above a streetcar, and Momma and the girl jumped back, startled. Momma put a calming hand on the girl's shoulder.

"Tell that boy some names have fire."

"You can put fire in a name?"

"Kwaku (KWAY-koo) storms in on a Wednesday,
and fire dances in Sagnika (sag-NEE-kah)!" Momma said.
"Names are that strong?" the girl asked.

"Xiomara (see-oh-MARR-ah) fights a battle in your mouth. Tongues bow to say Bilqis (bil-cKee-SS). Ju-long (JOO-longk) lunges like a dragon and Oudom (oo-DOM)... Oudom is..."

"Magnificent!" The girl's lips trembled.

"Yes, girl! Just like you!"

On her toes, the girl rose and kicked as they walked on.

"What about the kids at recess who said my name sounds made up?"

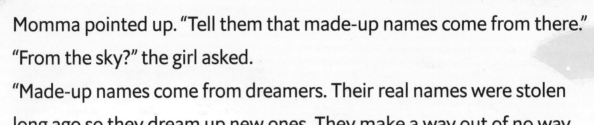

Momma pointed up. "Tell them that made-up names come from there."

"From the sky?" the girl asked.

"Made-up names come from dreamers. Their real names were stolen long ago so they dream up new ones. They make a way out of no way, make names out of no names—pull them from the sky!"

The girl reached up to pull names too. "Ta'jae (TAH-jay)...and Trayvon (tray-VAHN)...They sit on clouds with Jalonte (juh-LAHN-tay)!"

Momma nodded. "And Laquan (LAA-KWAHN) and Lamika (luh-MEE-kuh) are the twinkle in stars, the glimmer in minds that think and tinker."

"Are these names new songs?" the girl asked. "Yes, girl! Tell everybody to learn new songs too!" The girl twirled and leapt to the sky and they walked on.

The next day, the girl didn't want to go to school, but she had songs to teach.

"Line up!" Ms. Anderson (Mizzz AN-der-son) hollered.

The girl looked to the sky.

She saw dreams and fire there.

Ms. Anderson hollered names:

"Benjamin (BEN-juh-men)!"

TAP-ta-tap went the girl's feet.

"Here!"

"Siobhan (shih-VAHN)!" *ta-TAP*

"Here!"

"Olivia (o-LIV-ee-uh)!" *ta-TAP-ta-tap*

"Here!"

The girl stopped tapping.

Her name was getting stuck in Ms. Anderson's mouth again.

The girl sang. The whole class stared.

"What are you doing?" Ms. Anderson asked.

"I'm singing my name so you'll learn it."

"Names are not songs," Ms. Anderson huffed.

"Mizzz ANNN-der-sonnn," sang the girl.

Ms. Anderson frowned.

"Your name is a pretty song," said the girl.

Ms. Anderson's frown slowly turned into a smile.

"Why ... thank you."

"What about me?" Bob (BAWB) asked. "What's my song?"

The girl belted out, "BAW-AW-AW-AWBB!"
Other kids asked for songs too. She sang and sang their names.

Ms. Anderson asked, "Could we hear your song again?"

The girl sang her name.

The teacher sang it back. One kid sang it. Then another. And another.
Everyone sang her name: "KO-rah DJAAAA-lee-MOOOO-so!"

It was music to her ears.

GLOSSARY OF NAMES FEATURED IN THE STORY

Author's note: The glossary includes common pronunciations, but it doesn't mean the pronunciations will be correct for every person. Always listen carefully to how a person says their own name. Ask people how to pronounce their names and let them know that getting it right is important to you.

A video of the author pronouncing these names is available online at: www.theinnovationpress.com/yournameisasongvideo

AHLAM (AH-Hlam). Arabic origin. *Meaning*: Dreams.

ANDERSON (AN-der-son). English origin. *Meaning*: Son of Andrew.

BENJAMIN (BEN-juh-men). Hebrew origin. *Meaning*: Son of the right hand, son of strength, or son of the south.

BILQIS (bil-cKeeh-SS). Arabic origin. *Meaning*: Arabic name of the Queen of Sheba.

BOB (BAWB). English, Dutch origin. *Meaning*: Short form of Robert, from the Germanic Hrodebert, meaning "bright fame."

HA (HA). Vietnamese origin. *Meaning*: Sunshine, warmth.

JALONTE (juh-LAHN-tay). African American origin. Possibly a variant of Dante.

JU-LONG (JOO-longk). Chinese origin. *Meaning*: Huge, powerful dragon.

JUANA (HWAH-nah). Spanish origin. *Meaning*: Feminine form of Juan, God's gracious gift.

KORA-JALIMUSO (KO-rah-DJAA-lee MOO-so). Mandinka/West African origin. *Meaning*: The author created this name combination for the story's main character. Put together, it literally means harp of a female griot. A griot is someone who passes on oral history through song.

KOTONE (KOH-tow-neh). Japanese origin. *Meaning*: Sound of a koto, a harp-like musical instrument.

KWAKU (KWAY-koo). Akan/Ghana origin. *Meaning*: Born on a Wednesday.

LAMIKA (luh-MEE-kuh). African American origin. Variant of popular name, Tamika.

LAQUAN (LAA-KWAHN). African American origin. Combination of the popular name elements La and Quan.

MAMADOU (MAW-muh-DOO). West African variation of Muhammad. *Meaning*: Praiseworthy, the name of the prophet of Islam.

NGOZI (INN-GO-zee). Igbo/Nigerian origin. *Meaning*: Blessing.

OLIVIA (o-LIV-ee-uh). From multiple European ethnicities. *Meaning*: Feminine version of Oliver, which means elf army.

OLUMIDE (O-loo-muh-DAY). Yoruba/Nigerian/Benin origin. *Meaning*: My God has come.

OUDOM (oo-DOM). Khmer/Cambodian origin. *Meaning*: Magnificent, excellent.

SAGNIKA (sag-NEE-kah). Hindi/Sanskrit origin. *Meaning*: Associated with fire, possessing a sacred fire. Derived from Agni, the Sanskrit word for fire and the fire god of Hinduism.

SIOBHAN (shih-VAHN). Irish origin. Variant of Jeanne, Joan, of Hannah, or the Irish feminine version of John. *Meaning*: Gracious.

TA'JAE (TAH-jay). African American origin.

THANDOLWETHU (TAHN-dol-WEH-tooh). Northern Ndebele/South African/Zimbabwean origin. *Meaning*: Our love. It is also the name of a popular South African love song in the Xhosa language about a male heartbreaker.

TRAYVON (tray-VAHN). African American origin. The author included this name to honor the memory of Trayvon Martin, an innocent victim of gun violence.

XIOMARA (see-oh-MARR-ah). Spanish origin. *Meaning*: This name probably originates from the Germanic name Wigmar, which is formed with the words "wig," meaning war, and "meri," meaning famous.